Illustrations copyright © 1989 by Lena Anderson
Text copyright © 1991 by William Morrow & Company, Inc.
First published in Sweden in 1989 by
A.B. Rabén & Sjögren Bokförlag as *Stina och Stortruten*

First published in the United States
in 1991 by Greenwillow Books

Library of Congress Cataloging-in-Publication Data

Anderson, Lena.
Stina's visit
Translation of: Stina och Stortruten.
Summary: Stina and her grandfather visit
an old sailor on his birthday.
[1. Grandfathers—Fiction.
2. Birthdays—Fiction]   I. Title.
PZ7.A54393Sti
1991   [E]   90-2964
ISBN 0-688-09665-4.
ISBN 0-688-09666-2 (lib. bdg.)

LENA ANDERSON

STINA'S VISIT

Greenwillow Books

N E W   Y O R K

Every summer Stina visited her grandfather in his small gray house on an island. And every day she went to the beach, searching for things washed up by the sea.

"Look, Grandfather," called Stina. "This is
a good box. I can make a boat out of it."
"Indeed," said Grandfather.

"No, it's no good as a boat," Stina said sadly.
"It leaks."

"So I see," Grandfather said. "But come along, it's time
for lunch. I'll fry some fish."

One afternoon Grandfather looked at his calendar.
"Well, well," he said. "Today is Stretchit's birthday.
Why don't we go over and surprise him?"

"Who is Stretchit?" asked Stina.

"His real name is Axel," Grandfather said. "We've known each other ever since we were small children.

"It's good that I have a jar of honey," Grandfather said.
"Stretchit loves honey. We'll make honey sandwiches,
and we'll take a pot of coffee and some juice for you."

"And I'll take my box," Stina said. "We can
use it as a tray."

"Stretchit says that he lives on God's thumb,"
said Grandfather. "That's his house.
It's the farthest one out on the point.

"Stretchit says it's like living in Paradise."

When they got to the house, there was no sign of Stretchit.
"He must be somewhere,"   said Grandfather.

"He wasn't on the jetty," said Stina.
"Axel, where are you?" Grandfather called.

They opened the bedroom door—and there,
under the blanket, lay Stretchit. His eyes
were open. They looked shiny and sad.

"Stina and I have brought you a birthday surprise,"
Grandfather said. But Stretchit didn't move.

Stina put down the tray and went over to the bed.

Don't be sad," she said. "We've brought honey
sandwiches for you. Grandfather says you love
honey."

"He's right!" cried Stretchit,
and threw off his blanket.

"I thought everyone had forgotten me.
Now I will have a happy birthday!"

Stretchit ate one honey sandwich after another.
'This reminds me of one of my trips on a ship called
Pegasus, the time I won the big Honey Medal," he said.

"May I see the medal?" Stina asked.
"Unfortunately, it was blown into the sea during a
  dreadful storm off Cape Horn," Stretchit said.
"Indeed," said Grandfather.

"In the middle of the storm, believe it or not, a chest
came flying through the air. It landed with
a thud on the deck right in front of me.
It was full of gold and precious stones."

"May I see the chest?" asked Stina.
"Sorry," said Stretchit. "I lost it
  when the ship sank."
"Indeed," said Grandfather.

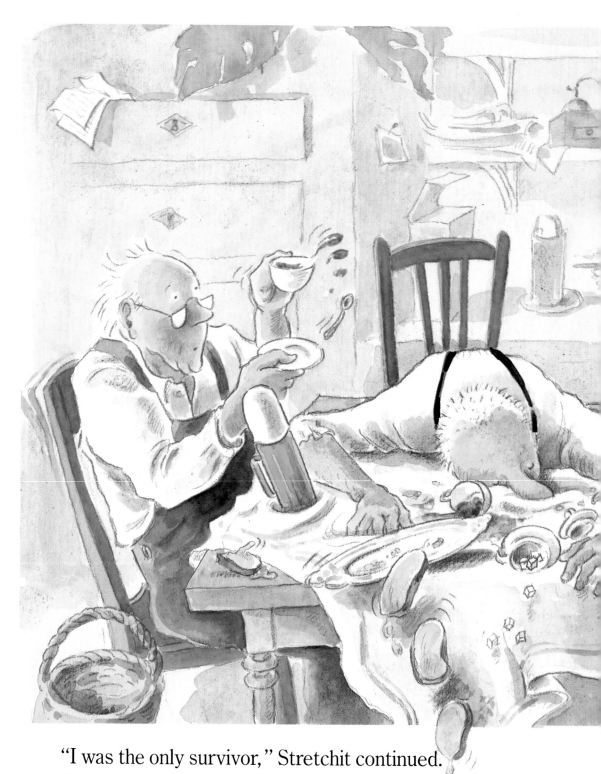

"I was the only survivor," Stretchit continued.
"I fought for my life in the raging waters of the Pacific.
The sea was alive with sharks.

"I thought my last moment had come, when a
   washtub came bobbing along."
"Indeed," said Grandfather.

"With my last strength, I managed to crawl into the tub.
I paddled for days and nights, and one glorious morning
I floated up on land, right here on God's thumb."
"Indeed," said Grandfather.

"May I see the tub?" asked Stina.
"It's right over there in the
cupboard," said Stretchit.

"What a good tub!" exclaimed Stina.
"You may have it. I don't need it anymore,"
   said Stretchit.

"Oh, thank you," said Stina.
"Mmmm," said Grandfather. "I think it's time
    for us to be getting home."

"Wait," cried Stretchit. He rushed back into his
bedroom and hopped under the blanket.

"Before you go, you must sing me a lullaby,"
he said. "For my birthday." As they sang,
Stretchit closed his eyes and went to sleep.

The next morning Stina tried out her new boat.
It didn't leak at all.

But she never could understand
how Stretchit had managed
to fit into it.